The Mole Sisters
and the Busy Bees

written and illustrated by Roslyn Schwartz

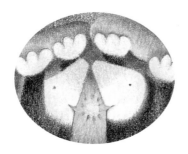

Annick Press Ltd.
Toronto • New York • Vancouver

Annick Press Ltd.

We acknowledge the support of the Canada Council for the Arts, the Ontario Arts Council, and the Government of Canada through the Book Publishing Industry Development Program (BPIDP) for our publishing activities.

Cataloging in Publication Data

Schwartz, Roslyn
        The mole sisters and the busy bees

ISBN 1-55037-663-2 (bound) ISBN 1-55037-662-4 (pbk.)

I. Title.

PS8587.C5785M632 2000   jC813'.54   C00-930583-1
PZ7.S4118Mo 2000

The art in this book was rendered in colored pencils.
The text was typeset in Apollo.

Distributed in Canada by: Published in the U.S.A. by Annick Press (U.S.) Ltd.
Firefly Books Ltd.   Distributed in the U.S.A. by:
3680 Victoria Park Avenue   Firefly Books (U.S.) Inc.
Willowdale, ON   P.O. Box 1338, Ellicott Station
M2H 3K1   Buffalo, NY 14205

Printed and bound in Canada by Kromar Printing Ltd., Winnipeg, Manitoba.

visit us at: **www.annickpress.com**

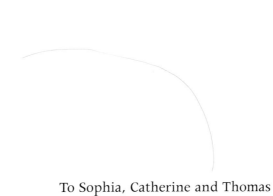

To Sophia, Catherine and Thomas

"Sometimes it's important to do nothing," said the mole sisters.

And that's what they
were doing …

under the tree

when along came a bee.

Bzzzzzzzzzzzzz.

"Busy busy busy,"
said the bee.

"What are you doing?" asked
the mole sisters.

"Can't stop," replied the bee.
"Too busy."

"Not us!" said the mole sisters.

And they followed him
out of the forest,

through the tall grass,

and into a meadow
full of flowers.

"How lovely," said the
mole sisters.

"Mmmm."

"Sniff-sniff."

"Mumble-bumble."

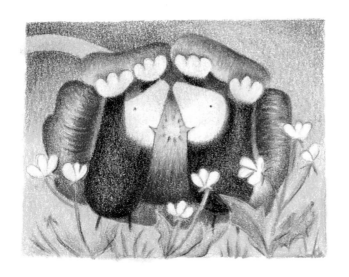

"BOO!!"

"Now we're as busy as bees!"

"And we look like flowers!"

Buzz Buzz Buzz Buzz

"They think we're flowers too!"

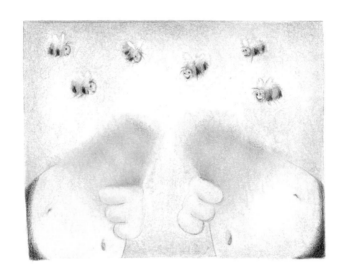

"AH-AH-AH——

TISHOOOO!"

"Bless you," said the bees.

"Thank you," said the mole sisters.

And they went back
to doing nothing,

just as they started out to do.

Also about the Mole Sisters: